The Dundee Cake:
A Saint Maggie Short Story

Books and Short Stories by Janet R Stafford

<u>Historical Fiction</u>
Saint Maggie (2011)
Walk by Faith: Saint Maggie Series Book 2 (2013)
A Time to Heal: Saint Maggie Series Book 3 (2014)
The Christmas Visitor: A Saint Maggie Short Story (2015)
Seeing the Elephant: Saint Maggie Series Book 4(2016)
The Enlistment: A Frankie Blaine Story (2017)

<u>Romance</u>
Heart Soul & Rock'n'Roll (2015)

The Dundee Cake:
A Saint Maggie Short Story

Janet R. Stafford

Squeaking Pips Press, Inc.
2016

ISBN 978-0-9992285-2-4

First Printing: 2016

Cover image of a Dundee cake is licensed from istockphoto.com

Squeaking Pips Press, Inc.
Hillsborough, NJ 08844

www.squeakingpips.com

Dedication

To Saint Maggie fans and friends:

Thank you!

Contents

Preface

While writing the Saint Maggie series, I have developed backstories for the characters. Some of these make it into the books themselves, but others call out to be told as a short story. This is one of the latter.

"The Dundee Cake" takes place during Christmas of 1852. Maggie is wrestling with sadness and loneliness brought on by the death of her husband John, son, and now John's aunt.

Financially strapped and battered by grief, Maggie endeavors to make Christmas a joyful time for her daughters and boarders only to realize that it will look nothing like Christmases past. She has little to spend on gifts for her daughters and even less to purchase the makings for Christmas dinner for the boarders.

Without Aunt Letty, running a rooming house was a backbreaking task. In desperation, Maggie hires Emily Johnson, a woman of color. As the two women become friends, Maggie learns that Emily is wrestling with deep sadness of her own, and this sets Maggie on a journey to ease her friend's suffering and to rediscover the joy of Christmas in her new circumstances.

I started writing "The Dundee Cake" while sitting outside at Peddler's Village, Lahaska, PA. I was part of a group of more than thirty authors, and each weekend, two to four of us would take turns selling and signing our work. One day, I was sitting outside, as usual. Although it was late May, the temperature soared to over ninety degrees Fahrenheit. I hid under an umbrella, covered myself with sunscreen and a hat, and gulped down a variety of liquids, but to no avail. So, it doesn't surprise me in the least that I began to write a Christmas story!

I had fun writing Lydia and Frankie as children, and going back to the beginning of Maggie and Emily's friendship. But more importantly, I wanted to show the power of love and generosity.

I hope you enjoy reading this Saint Maggie prequel. It's got a very nineteenth-century Christmas tone to it, so draw close to the fire and read it aloud to one another.

Janet R. Stafford

The Dundee Cake

MAGGIE BEATTY BLAINE used to love Christmas. Ever since her 1840 marriage to John Blaine, the couple had celebrated by going to church Christmas morning, having a celebratory dinner at home, doing a kindness to a neighbor or a stranger, and concluding the day by singing carols around the piano.

She had been nineteen years old in 1840. Her pale skin had glowed, her hazel eyes were bright, and her auburn hair glossy. She was young, innocent, and full of hope.

But now it was December 1852. She felt much older than her thirty-one years and oh, so weary. For on February 20th of 1850, she had lost her beloved John and their dear little son Gideon. Now, almost three years later, the shadows of those losses crept steadily upon her as Christmas approached.

It was, in fact, only a few days away. This time Maggie not only was facing the third holiday without John and Gideon, but also the first without Aunt Letty, John's aunt. The older woman had been her rock and was the one who had advised her to start a boarding house. Side by side they energetically had tackled the backbreaking tasks of feeding four male boarders, keeping the house clean, and handling the laundry and mending. But in June, Aunt Letty suddenly passed away from heart failure at the age of fifty-eight. Now life for Maggie was a grim, exhausting struggle.

Somehow, though, she managed to maintain a bright countenance for the sake of her daughters, ten-year-old Lydia and six-year-old Frances, also known as Frankie. Maggie wanted to make the holiday meaningful and joyful for her collection of solitary male boarders, too. They consisted of Grandpa O'Reilly, a man of no defined job who scraped to bring something resembling rent to Maggie every week; writer Chester Carson whose best days seemed to be behind him; and two young apprentice lawyers, Geoffrey Illington, and Lucius Kemp.

Sadly, Maggie was not much of a landlady when it came to making money. She could have found men with the wherewithal to pay her both weekly and well. But every one of the boarders had come to her hungry, cold, lost or helpless, and the idea of turning them away horrified her. The Methodist Maggie took seriously Jesus' teachings, particularly the one that said that whoever fed the hungry, gave drink to the thirsty, welcomed the stranger, clothed the naked, cared for the sick, or visited the imprisoned did the same for him. Thus, she unfailingly saw Jesus in all who came to her door, welcomed them to her rooming house, and took them into her family. She may not have been paid in cash, but she was richly compensated in love and respect.

The trouble was love and respect did not pay her bills.

*

It was not yet time to start the noon dinner and since she had finished scrubbing the kitchen and hall floors, Maggie retreated to her bedroom for a few minutes of solitude and rest.

Wrapping her shawl close, she took a seat on the chair in front of her writing desk, opened its drawer, and took out her journal. She had started writing a journal after the death of her loved ones. Somehow it helped to fill the pages with her sorrows, her hopes, her fears, her joys, and her prayers.

Maggie opened the book to the last entry. A blank page was next to it. She picked up her pen, dipped it in the inkwell, and began to write on the fresh page.

December 20, 1852

Early this morning I sat and looked out one of the front parlor windows. The sky was like lead and snow sifted gently down like flour. The window affords a fine view of Blaineton's square and the houses and streets surrounding it. At that hour, all was peaceful and sleepy, as if the world were ever a quiet place. But it is not. If it were, I would be welcoming the approach of Christmas rather than dreading it.

Many of the houses on the square were built in the middle of the last century. John's ancestors, the founders of Blaineton, lived across the way from this one. It grew from a humble dwelling to a building with two floors and a new wing. People unrelated live there now. John's family moved to a large new house on the southern outskirts when their carriage manufactory became prosperous.

My people never lived in the town at all. We started out on a little farm north of Blaineton. In the last century, our people were far from well-to-do. Until they too started a carriage business, it was a hardscrabble existence for them, and they were well-versed in tragedy and loss.

I wonder how long their hearts ached after each sad event.

I want to be brave, Journal. I want to be resilient but, oh, I still miss my John and our little Gideon so. And now dear Aunt Letty is gone. All I do these days is work until my hands are raw and my back aches. I worry whether I'll be able to pay the bills. My boarders, God bless them, are good-hearted, and pay rent when they can, but it never seems enough to cover all the expenses. Most nights I cry because I do not know what to do or where to turn. I fear my courage and strength have been shattered along with my complacent belief that life would be untroubled.

For comfort I read the Bible 'til my eyes can take no more and pray until I fall asleep. I search for something, anything that resembles solace, but when solace comes it never stays long.

And now Christmas is nearly upon us once again.

Dear Lord, I have nothing to give my daughters. Nothing! I cannot even purchase enough yarn to knit hats or stockings or mittens for them. And there is barely money to feed my boarders. I cannot purchase a Christmas goose nor the fruits necessary for the Dundee cake. What shall I do?

Please help me, Lord. You were born in poverty. You lived in poverty. You died a criminal. You've known far worse than I ever will know. O, help me find a way, my Jesus. Help me find a way.

With a sigh, Maggie blotted the page and closed the book. Then she got up and went downstairs to help Emily start dinner.

*

In September, Maggie had found herself exhausted trying to shoulder the heavy work of a boarding house on her own. So, she looked for help. She ended up hiring Emily Johnson to help with the cooking and cleaning. Emily was as tall as Maggie but with skin the color of milky hot chocolate, deep brown hair, and amber eyes. She usually braided her hair, collecting the braids into a bun at the back of her head. When they had heavy work to do, she would wear a scarf, something Maggie also did to stay tidy.

Emily was shy at first, keeping her eyes down and doing her work with nary a word. But every day after the noon dinner dishes were done, Maggie would sit down and have a cup of tea for a brief rest. And every day she would invite Emily to join her. And every day Emily would sit quietly and sip her tea, while Maggie talked and asked questions which Emily answered with one or two words. Eventually, the darker woman's shyness melted, and she began to speak in full sentences.

Three months later, though, Maggie still did not know much of Emily's life apart from her work at the Second Street Boarding House. She did learn that Emily was married to a man named Nate, short for Nathaniel and that he had a carpenter shop on Depot Street. Maggie also discovered that Emily's mother had brought her north from Maryland. Since Maryland was a slave state, Maggie wondered if Emily's mother was a free woman or an escaped slave. If a slave, she wondered what privations the woman had faced bringing herself and her baby to freedom. Since Emily had said nothing more, the answers remained shrouded.

Like some Methodists, Maggie was an abolitionist. Her one luxury was a subscription to a newspaper called *The National Era*, a weekly antislavery publication from Washington, DC. During her infrequent spare time, she devoured it and had read with great interest a serialized story by Harriet Beecher Stowe called "Uncle Tom's Cabin." In March of 1852, the tale was printed in novel form, and everyone seemed to be talking about it. Since Maggie did not have the money to buy the book, she was pleased to read the story in serial form and was prepared to comment should someone ask her. No one ever did, though.

Maggie long had been against slavery, but after reading *Uncle Tom's Cabin*, she had become passionately abolitionist. In her eyes enslaved people were men and women and children of God. It was beyond her comprehension that one group of people would treat another as a commodity and not as fellow human beings.

Now she glanced at Emily as they put together a noon dinner of canned green beans and fatback, cornbread, stewed tomatoes, ham, and eggs. Once again, Maggie wondered about Emily's mother and once again chose not to say anything. But to make conversation she said, "I hope this is enough cornbread." She pulled a pan out of the oven.

"And I hope some of those men pay you their rent," Emily replied. "Mrs. Blaine, you know you can't provide room and board on thin air." Emily was nothing if not practical.

"I know," the other woman sighed. "And please call me Maggie. Although I pay you, we do work side by side."

Emily smiled slightly. "Very well, Maggie." And, with a wicked little grin, she added, "And you may call me Mrs. Johnson."

Wide-eyed, Maggie nearly dropped the pan. "Is that what you wish? We can be more formal if –"

And Emily collapsed into chuckles. "I'm just joking! It's Emily and nothing more." She fetched a basket of eggs from the table. "And you're right. We do work side by side." She paused, basket in hand. "I like that. I haven't really known any white people. You're not what I expected."

"I haven't really known any colored people," Maggie responded, blushing. "Shall we be friends?"

"I'd like that."

Setting the pan of cornbread aside to cool, Maggie turned to face her new friend. "May I confide in you? My situation is this: Grandpa O'Reilly has no money to speak of. Mr. Carson tries his best but has only sold one or two stories these past two months."

Emily began cutting breakfast's leftover ham into pieces. "What about that Mr. Illington and Mr. Kemp?"

Maggie dismissed the idea with a wave of her hand. "Oh, they're boys! They might be given a Christmas gift of money from their employer, but it's uncertain. I don't know much about the lawyer they work for, but I do know this: he pays very little."

Emily heaved a sigh. "Isn't that the way. He figures they're apprentices so it's all right if they starve."

"I'm afraid that's true."

Maggie went to the dining room and began to lay the table, all the while ruminating as she worked. She was frugal to the extreme, carefully counting every penny to make sure she had enough to pay Emily every week and still cover as much of her bills as possible. Emily's wages were not a great deal. She paid her friend seventy-five cents a week. Maggie made up for it by seeing that her new friend partook of dinner with the rest of the boarding house and carried home supper for two.

As usual, there was no answer to her dilemma, except prayer and hope. Upon reminding herself that worry never solved a solitary thing, Maggie returned to the kitchen just as her daughters blew in the back door.

"Mama!" Little Frankie threw her arms around her mother's waist with the unabashed love only a child can have.

Maggie embraced her daughter and kissed the top of her red-haired head. As she released her, Maggie saw that Frankie's scarf was askew. Her coat was half-unbuttoned and soaking wet. "Egad, Frances," she exclaimed. "What happened to you?"

"Snowball fight," Lydia answered.

Of her two daughters, Frankie was most like Maggie had been as a child. Maggie had preferred running races with the boys and climbing trees to sitting in the parlor and learning how to sew. She had chafed at the restrictive bit of a "girl's place" and knew that Frankie would do the same. So, she did not push her daughter to conform to the usual expectations. Maggie was not sure whether she was taking the right approach, but her heart wouldn't let her do otherwise.

"With whom did you have the snowball fight?" she asked.

"The boys," Frankie replied. "The boys" were a gang of three youngsters who didn't seem to notice that Frankie was a girl, which was just fine with the little redhead. "I won, too!"

"Did you?" Maggie chuckled. "Well, good for you!"

Having resolved that, Maggie turned to greet her older daughter with a hug and kiss.

Lydia responded by snuggling up and holding her mother tightly. At the age of ten, Lydia was bright, studious, devoted, and nearly unflappable. She reminded Maggie of a combination of John Blaine and her mother, Deborah Livingston Beatty.

"I love you, Liddy," Maggie whispered into her ear.

Frankie overheard. "Do you love me, too?"

Maggie released Lydia and gave her youngest a peck on the nose. "Always and forever!" Her daughters were the only bright light in her life, something for which she was ever grateful. "Now, why don't you both get ready for dinner? We'll be calling the men soon."

*

It always struck Maggie as odd that dinner took so long to prepare and yet was dispensed with so quickly. Once sated, the men rose from the table and returned to their respective vocations, her girls trundled off to school, and Maggie and Emily were left with a pile of dishes to clean.

As usual, they tackled the task with energy and efficiency. But after everything was put away, they always had a little time on their hands, during which they would sit and take a cup of tea.

Maggie was lonely for female companionship and looked forward to these few moments of relaxation with her new friend. Letty had been close to her, so close that Maggie always felt that she could tell her aunt anything. Now that Letty was gone, she yearned to have that type of relationship again.

Although it was still too early to tell what kind of a friend the dark-skinned woman sitting across from her would be, Maggie was encouraged by what she could see. Emily's eyes were kind and, when joking, sparkled impishly, which Maggie found appealing. Emily had the potential to be a close friend, even though they were not the same color. Maggie took a sip of tea. As she set the cup down, she said, "How long have you and Nate been married?"

Emily smiled. "Seven years. How long were you married?"

"Just short of ten years." With a sad sigh, Maggie added, "John died of scarlet fever. Our son Gideon contracted it first and then John followed suit. It's unusual for an adult to get it, so when John took ill he thought it was only a sore throat and continued working. Then suddenly..." Maggie took a deep breath. "Then suddenly it was just too late."

Emily's expression softened. "Your boy died, too, didn't he?"

Eyes averted, Maggie nodded.

"I'm sorry." After a moment's silence, Emily unexpect-
edly cried out, "Oh, Maggie! I hope you don't mind, but I
need to tell you something! It's just eating me up inside. I
don't understand how it could have happened. He would
have been born about this time, you see. Why did he have
to come early? I thought everything was all right. He made
it past the first three months. Why couldn't he go to term?"

Confused, Maggie said, "Who?"

"My baby. He came too soon. He didn't have a chance."
Emily swallowed. "I don't know why, Maggie, but Nate and
I just can't have a child."

"I'm so sorry." Maggie had suffered a miscarriage be-
tween Lydia and Frankie and was no stranger to the pain
that came when the promise of a child, a child one loved
even though one couldn't see it, was abruptly cut off.

"We lost three others over the years. I never seem to be
able to bring them to term."

Reaching across the table, Maggie laid her hand over
Emily's clenched fist and gave it a gentle squeeze.

Eyes brimming Emily turned her gaze from the table
to Maggie. "It must be me. I must be doing something
wrong."

"You're doing nothing wrong." Maggie said quickly, although she was familiar with the heartbreak and self-
recrimination.

"It's just sometimes... sometimes I think God is pun-
ishing us."

"Oh, no!" Maggie squeezed Emily's hand again. "He's
not. I promise you."

The other woman laughed bitterly. "How can you be so
sure?"

"Because I know God cares for us as deeply as he cares
for the sparrows. I know every hair on our head is precious
to him. Why would a God who loves like that punish you
this way, and for something you don't even know you did,
if indeed you did anything at all?"

12

"Then why does he let things like this happen? It's not right!" Emily put her free hand to her face and began to weep.

"Oh, my dear, don't..."

"I can't help it," Emily sobbed. "I just hurt so bad inside. Why do these things happen?"

Touched, Maggie began to weep with her as she held Emily's hand. She had often asked herself the same thing: why did God let John die? Why did God let Gideon die? And Letty? It wasn't fair. It wasn't fair at all. And yet it happened all the time.

*

That night Maggie sat on her girls' bed and loosened, brushed, and re-braided their hair. It was the usual evening ritual and it gave her an opportunity to talk with them.

She was working on Frankie, whose unruly red masses seemed to knot even when arranged in two plaits, a rather impressive feat had it not so difficult to correct. Maggie wished Frankie's hair had come in straight and smooth, like Lydia's. She gritted her teeth as she struggled to get the brush through.

Frankie squeaked, "Ow!"

"I'm sorry. But if you would just hold still, it wouldn't hurt."

"But it hurts *before* I move." Frankie pouted.

With a sigh, Maggie stopped worked and gently stroked her daughter's hair. "I will try not to tug. I promise."

Lip still protruding, Frankie nodded her assent.

Maggie went back to work. "Today Mrs. Johnson told me something very sad."

"What is it, Mama?" Hair braided for the night and dressed in her nightgown, Lydia was sitting on the other side of the bed.

"She told me that she and Mr. Johnson were going to have a baby, but it came too early and died."

Lydia frowned. "Why does that happen, Mama?"

"I don't know, Liddy."

Her eldest was quiet for a moment. Then she blurted, "I wish all babies could live, Mama, and their mothers, too. It's not right!"

"I agree." Maggie sighed. "This happened to Mrs. Johnson about three months ago and she is still very sad."

"But it's almost Christmas," Frankie said. "How can anyone be sad at Christmastime?"

The question nearly broke her mother's heart. How? Tragedy and grief were no respecters of human celebrations. Maggie began to braid her daughter's hair. "Sometimes people are sad at Christmas, Frankie, even though it is a happy season. Sad things happen, and they can't see the joy for their sadness. Grieving takes time."

"Then maybe we should do something kind for Mr. and Mrs. Johnson," Lydia suggested. "Maybe it would cheer them up a little."

"Why, that is an excellent idea!" Maggie took the piece of rag sitting beside her and tied it to the end of Frankie's braid. "What do you think we should do?"

Frankie bit her lip in thought. "We could bake something."

"Molasses cookies," Lydia exclaimed.

"And gingerbread! Everybody loves gingerbread!"

"Wonderful. I'll see what we have in our stores and tomorrow we'll make their gift." Maggie scooted back on the mattress and lay back on the pillows. She opened her arms. "Come here, my kind-hearted darlings! I love you both so very much." They snuggled with her and she held them tight. "I'm proud of you for thinking of others. And your father would be proud of you, too."

After a moment, Frankie asked, "Are you still sad about Papa and Gideon, Mama?"

"Yes, I am," Maggie said quietly.

"And Aunt Letty?"

"Yes. I'm sad about her, too."

Lydia sat up at looked down on her mother. "I didn't know that, Mama. Are you sad all the time?"

"No, not all the time. I find joy every time I see your faces. However, I don't want you two to worry. I am strong, and I'll be just fine. Now why don't I read a story from the Bible? Then we'll have our prayers and put out the lamps."

*

When Maggie had been a child one of the big Christmas treats was a Dundee cake. Her forebears had come from Scotland and brought with them the tradition of making a light-colored fruitcake decorated on top with concentric circles of almonds. Christmas dinner was not Christmas dinner without a Dundee cake.

This year, however, as Maggie made a shopping list, she wondered if she could afford to bake one. The ingredients were rich: raisins both dark and gold, currants, candied orange peel, a lemon, and almonds. She had milk, eggs and flour, enough sugar, and in the back of the cupboard an old bottle of whiskey. Being temperance, Maggie kept alcohol only for baking a Dundee cake and for putting into her sore throat and cough remedies.

But she didn't know if she afford all those lovely fruits.

Maggie retreated to her bedroom and fetched the old tin that held the household money. Then she took it to her escritoire and opened the tin, spilling its contents on to the desktop. It wasn't very much and didn't take long to count. Once she paid the green grocer and the butcher's bills, gave Emily her seventy-five cents, there would be little left over for a goose, let alone for Dundee cake fixings.

Dear Lord, she prayed, *help me be less concerned with the details of Christmas and more with its greater joy.*

With that, she swept the coins back into the tin and returned it to its hiding place in her chest of drawers.

*

After surveying her supplies in the cupboards and the root cellar, Maggie adjudged that she had enough molasses, sugar, ginger, milk, butter, and flour to make three gingerbread cakes and several dozen molasses cookies.

"That's that," she murmured. "Well, so be it. We will put joy into what we make however humble it may be."

That evening she set everything out on the kitchen table and went to work with Lydia and Frankie.

Delighted to be making sweets, the girls giggled and chattered and teased each other. Their joy was contagious and for the first time in what felt like ages, Maggie laughed honestly, unburdened by the sadness and trouble that constantly gnawed at her heart.

They had just removed the first batch from the oven when the two young attorneys-in-training swept into the kitchen.

Mr. Illington cried, "What is this we smell? Cookies!"

"May we have some?" Mr. Kemp now lingered a bit too close to the table where the first batch of cookies was cooling.

"No, you may not have some!" Lydia positioned herself protectively in front of the delicacies. "This is for Mr. and Mrs. Johnson!"

"Yeah!" Frankie took her place at the table too, presenting the young men with a diminutive but fierce barrier. "Leave our cookies alone."

"Now, now," Maggie soothed. "We have enough for them to have one or two cookies each." She gazed at the eager men. They were not quite out of their teens.

However, they had learned enough self-control not to attempt to steal a snack later. Naughty boys of fourteen might try to do it, but not attorney apprentices. Maggie assumed a stern visage. "However, you may not have them until Christmas Day."

Illington sighed. "But Mrs. Blaine, that's three whole days from now!"

"And it will pass quickly, I promise." She smiled now. "Although, if you're still hungry, I will make you some bread and butter. We have plenty of that and coffee left over from supper, as well."

"Well, I guess if we can't have gingerbread, then we'll just have to take plain old bread and butter and a cup of coffee," Kemp said, making the best of it. "Thank you, Mrs. Blaine."

"You're welcome. Why don't you go into the dining room? I'll bring it to you."

"It'll only take two shakes of a lamb's tail," Frankie chirped, parroting something she had heard Aunt Letty say.

The child's words reminded Maggie that Aunt Letty was still very much with them. She showed up in the phrases she had taught Lydia and Frankie, the way she had trained Maggie to care for the boarding house, the spirit of love and acceptance present in it, and in so much more.

As for John Blaine, Maggie saw him every time she looked at her girls. Frankie had his green eyes and boundless energy, and Lydia had his nose and ears, long limbs and height.

I know I'll see you in Heaven, Maggie told her missing loved ones. *But for now, you're with me in spirit, and I'm grateful.*

*

Two days before Christmas, Maggie and the girls chose a gingerbread cake and a couple dozen molasses cookies, wrapped them in tea towels and put them in a basket.

It was a warm day for late December, which made for a pleasant walk up Second Street to Depot Street.

After a few carefully chosen questions Maggie had learned that Emily and Nate did not live on Water Street where most of the town's black population lived. Emily had told her that the best they could afford was an old run-down shack at the end of Depot Street.

Nate, however, had rolled up his sleeves and refurbished the shack to create a cozy shop up front and a small apartment in the back.

The houses along Depot Street were not prosperous, which explained why the Johnsons could afford a building there. In fact, as Maggie walked along with her girls, she noticed that a few of the dwellings were in poor condition. Either their residents did not have enough money to keep them in good repair or they did not care if their homes collapsed about their ears.

But Maggie was not prepared for what met her eyes at the very end of the street.

She hoped that she might be wrong, that perhaps she was looking at the wrong house. But she knew she was not.

The very last structure on the street was the Johnson's house, and it was a wreck of a building. Clearly it recently had suffered a fire that destroyed the back and had left the front on the verge of collapse.

There was no question who lived in the dwelling, for a sign out front proclaimed, "Carpentry. Nate Johnson."

"Oh, dear me," Maggie whispered.

"Is that where Mr. and Mrs. Johnson live?" Confused, Lydia looked from the shack to Maggie. "Did they have a fire?" Mama, what happened to their house?

"I don't know, dear. Let's see if anyone is inside. Perhaps they have moved and are living with family or friends now." Maggie strode to the door and knocked firmly, but not too firmly, as she was afraid everything might come toppling down.

In a few seconds, the door creaked open. Behind it was a tall man. Strong of arm and broad-chested, his skin was dark brown and his short hair black. Maggie knew at once that he was Nate.

"May I help you?" he said, eyeing the trio with suspicion.

"I am Maggie Blaine. Emily works for me, and my daughters and I thought we would bring you a cake and some cookies for Christmas."

At this, Nate's expression softened. "Thank you kindly." He hesitated, but then added, "Won't you please come in?"

As they stepped into the dimly lit room, Emily rose from her seat by the fireplace.

The couple had done their best to make the carpentry shop a home, but it was rugged. They had managed to save a few pieces of furniture from the fire: a mattress covered with a tired quilt served as a bed; a cooking pot; an iron frying pan; and assorted utensils. On the mantle were a smattering of plates, cups, and silverware. A hastily constructed table, with no tablecloth, and two mismatched chairs occupied the middle of the room.

Clearly embarrassed, Emily rushed to the table as Maggie set the basket upon it. "Oh, I wish you hadn't come! I didn't want you to see what happened to us."

"What you had was a fire," Maggie replied as if it was nothing. "Fires are a regular occurrence. How did yours happen?"

Frowning, Nate muttered, "Someone didn't appreciate us living on this street. We're all in the same boat when it comes to money here, but they touched a torch to our place in the middle of the night to teach us a lesson. We woke up to smoke and flames."

"A few of the neighbors helped us stop the fire from going too far, though," Emily said. "Maggie, we lost a lot, and we don't have the money to replace it yet."

The Johnsons had scavenged what they could to make the place semi-habitable. Half-burnt boards had been nailed up to create a back wall for the shop. Despite the holes and chinks plugged with newspaper and other rescued wood, Maggie still could feel the wind finding its way in. The building had to be uncomfortable on a cold day and icy at night.

"How come no one helped you fix it up?" Frankie asked. "People always do that after a fire."

Emily squatted before the child and looked her in the face. "Honey, we're colored. Folks on this street put the fire out because they didn't want it to spread to their own homes. We got a little help later from members of our church once they heard but..." She sighed. "Well, let's just say sometimes it's not possible to fix things right away."

Lydia frowned. "That's not right. You shouldn't be living here. *Someone* should help you."

Emily smiled wearily. "Who?" She stood up.

"Who?" Maggie replied. "Why, us, of course."

Nate frowned again. "You?"

Maggie turned to the basket, removed the wrapped cookies and placed them on the table. "Yes. Us. As my daughter said, someone should help. And since we are here, that someone is us. Please have a cookie."

Nate hesitated, then picked one up and bit into it.

"They're molasses," Frankie piped up.

"My favorite!" Emily picked up a cookie now. "Why don't you all have one with us?"

"Thank you." But Lydia's smile vanished as Frankie's hand grabbed the biggest cookie on the plate. "Frances!"

Chagrined, Frankie put the sweet back and chose a smaller one.

Reaching out, Maggie took Emily's hand. "I am helping you because someone helped me in my time of need. John and I eloped, much to our families' disapproval, and we were both disowned. We had no place to live. Fortunately, John's Aunt Letty did not care what people thought and took us into her home. When John died, she helped me turn her house into a boarding house. We don't have much at Second Street, but we do have two rooms to spare on the second floor of the new wing. Please use one for a bedroom and the other for a sitting room. No one will be upstairs to disturb you. My daughters and I sleep on the first floor and all my boarders live in the old section of the house. Unless I suddenly acquire one or two more boarders, you will have that floor all to yourselves."

"You would do that for us?" Nate's tone was incredulous.

"Yes. And you may stay as long as you wish. Room and board will be free since Emily works with me."

An astounded Emily sought for words. "But Maggie... are you sure? I mean, you have so little. Don't you don't want something in the way of rent?"

Maggie adamantly shook her head. "No. Only perhaps a bit of help from Nate when something needs fixing."

"I could do that happily," he said. "But, Mrs. Blaine, we're colored."

"And I'm white, and so what?

"So what? Folk burned our house, that's what."

"Ah, but no one would dare burn a house on the town square," Maggie replied with a mischievous little smile. "And besides, I could always say I have live-in help."

He chuckled. "You know, I think I like you."

Maggie smiled. "And I think I like you, too."

Nate's eyes began to glisten with tears. "I've been praying for a miracle, Mrs. Blaine. Em has been mighty cold these past few weeks. I don't care about myself, but I'd welcome having her living in a nice safe, clean place." He took a breath and then his face relaxed. "I'll be able to do my carpentry here and when I earn enough, maybe I can buy a shop over on Water Street."

"That sounds like an excellent plan," Maggie said.

At this, Frankie began jumping up and down. "Hooray! You're going to live with us!"

"We'll help you pack," Lydia added.

"Oh, honey, there's hardly anything *to* pack," Emily said, as she laughed around her tears. "Why don't I make us all some tea first, so we can enjoy those lovely cookies? Then we'll worry about packing."

*

While Nate and Emily were upstairs getting settled in their rooms, Maggie called the boarders to the kitchen to give them with the news.

She put the kettle on and brought one of the gingerbread cakes to the table. As she sliced it and set the pieces on plates, she related the whole story. "And so," she concluded, "we shall have two new people living in our house."

Mr. Carson calmly lit his pipe. "I would expect nothing less of you, Mrs. Blaine, given Mr. and Mrs. Johnson's situation."

"But what will the town say?" Mr. Kemp asked as Maggie placed a piece of cake before him. He picked up his fork. "I mean, they are colored."

Grandpa frowned. "Don't you worry about them, lad! All anyone has to know is that Mrs. Blaine has hired two new workers."

"It's none of their business, anyway," Lydia primly added. "It's Mama's house and she may run it as she pleases."

Maggie smiled at her eldest daughter. "That's very true. And in this house, we live according to Jesus' rule: treat others as we would have them treat us."

"Aye, it never hurts to be kind," Grandpa said. "No matter what others may think of you."

"Speaking of kindness," Mr. Illington said, "we have received a Christmas gift from our employer. Mr. Kemp and I wish to give all of it to you, Mrs. Blaine." He reached into his pocket and laid a packet before her.

"And I did a few odd jobs for the pastor and Dr. Lightner," Grandpa added, slapping some coins on the table. "It ain't much, but it's yours, me daughter."

Mr. Carson smiled as he puffed on his pipe. "Well, it seems I have been paid in full for both of my stories." He too placed money on the table. "That should take care of the past two months' rent and the coming month, as well."

Maggie was speechless, but Frankie was not. "Look at all that money, Mama! We're rich!"

"Frances, don't be rude."

"Now we can have a goose *and* a Dundee cake for Christmas dinner!"

"Count it, Mama," Lydia urged.

Maggie hesitated

Mr. Carson said, "Yes, do count it, please. We are honored to give it to you and wish to know how much you have."

So, Maggie counted and did indeed have enough to pay for a fine Christmas dinner, her bill at the butcher and green grocer's shops, and even some sweets for her daughters. Tears filled her eyes as she said, "Thank you all. You are so kind, and God has blessed us greatly." And then a thought occurred to her. "However, this money can give us momentary pleasure." She took a breath and added, "Or it can have a more lasting impact. Mr. and Mrs. Johnson have little but the clothing on their backs. Also, many of Mr. Johnson's tools were destroyed in the fire. How would you feel about using most of this money to help them and use the rest to pay off the boarding house bills?"

Frankie's lower lip formed a pout. "Do you mean we won't have our Christmas dinner after all?"

"Oh, we'll have Christmas dinner," Maggie said, "never fear! But we will have chicken instead of goose and one of our gingerbread cakes for dessert."

"No Dundee cake?"

"No, Frankie. We shall give that up to help someone else."

Frankie continued her pouting for a moment. Finally, she muttered, "All right, if we must."

"Yes, we must," Lydia agreed. "Of course, we must! It's the right thing to do."

The men nodded and murmured their assent.

"Well done, everyone," Grandpa said. "After all, Christmas isn't our birthday, is it? It's the birthday of him who was born poor and in a stable at that and who taught us to love and help others, especially the poorest among us."

Mr. Carson smiled as he puffed on his pipe. "And what better way to spend our money than to make this a happy Christmas for Mr. and Mrs. Johnson?"

"Thank you." Maggie sat back in her chair. "Bless you all."

"No, Mrs. Blaine," Mr. Carson said. "Bless *you.*"

*

Maggie's Journal, 23 December 1852

How odd that giving something up should make me feel so joyful! But Grandpa is right. Christmas is not about us, it is about love.

The men went out this afternoon with Nate and helped him select the items he needs to do his carpentry. Furthermore, the pastor of his church has offered him a space in the old barn on Water Street, the place in which their African Methodist Episcopal Church worships. It is a perfect location for Nate and will remove him from Depot Street, where he and his shop might be molested again.

When they returned to the boarding house, Nate showed us all his new tools as if he were a child displaying his Christmas toys. And I knew then that we have done the right thing.

As for Emily... oh, Journal! Her eyes lit up when we entered the dry goods store! There we purchased enough cloth and thread to make two new dresses and sundries for her as well as two pair of trousers, three shirts, and sundries for Nate. I cannot explain the joy that washed over me as the two of us began to cut and sew the new items.

Best of all, joy has not deserted me! God has shown me the way. I know I always will miss my John and Gideon and our Aunt Letty, but I know now that happiness and joy will come and visit and after a time, will stay forever.

*

On Christmas morning most of the boarding house family went to the little Methodist church to which Maggie belonged for the holy day's worship. Upon returning home, Maggie, Emily, and the girls made the promised Christmas dinner: two roasted chickens, bread stuffing, canned corn, canned beans, a cranberry relish, two loaves of bread, and butter.

Maggie had planned to serve a gingerbread cake with whipped cream for dessert, but as she was about to rise to clear the table for the dessert course, Mr. Carson held up a hand. "Please excuse me, and don't do anything until I return." With that he serenely stood and walked out of the dining room, leaving Maggie in a state of mild confusion.

"Please excuse us, too," Mr. Kemp said, and then he and Mr. Illington left the room.

"And me, as well," said Grandpa.

Bewildered, Maggie met Emily and Nate's eyes. "What's going on?"

"I have no idea," Emily replied.

But Maggie could see both she and her husband were working very hard not to crack a smile.

In the next instant, all four boarders re-entered the dining room singing "Joy to the World" at the top of their voices. Last in line was Mr. Carson, who was bearing a tray upon which sat a Dundee cake.

Maggie's hands flew to her mouth.

Frankie and Lydia leapt up and proceeded to dance around the little procession.

"A Dundee cake?" Maggie gasped.

Mr. Carson set it before her with a flourish. "The gentlemen of the house had a chat after you went to the dry goods store. We decided to do something for you since you do so much for us."

"But how?" Maggie said.

"We pooled our resources, of course." Mr. Carson nodded in Nate's direction. "Mr. and Mrs. Johnson contributed, too. A few pennies here and a few pennies there added up.

"I then went to see Miss Amelia Barnett. She was about to close her tea shop for the day, but I prevailed upon her to do a favor for us and bake on short notice. When I explained what you had done for Mr. and Mrs.

Johnson, and indeed for us all, she was more than happy to comply, even though we did not have enough to pay the full cost of the cake.

"You see, Miss Barnett remembers a time when she was ill. You brought her enough soup to feed her for days and you stopped by every day to care for her and do chores about her house. You are, Mrs. Blaine, well-loved by those who have eyes to see and ears to hear."

"Oh..." Speechless, Maggie looked from one face to the other. Finally, she found her voice. "Oh, thank you! Thank you all!"

And it was as if she could feel the presence of John, and Gideon, and Aunt Letty, and all those she had loved and who no longer were present on earth. And then she didn't feel alone, not anymore. She lifted up and blessed by the love and good wishes of a great cloud of family and friends.

"Merry Christmas, Mama!" Lydia kissed her on the cheek.

"Yes, Merry Christmas," Frankie chirped, throwing her arms around her mother. "Can we cut the cake now?"

Heart full, Maggie laughed. "Yes! Yes, let's do."

But she kept her arms around Frankie just a bit longer as she gazed fondly upon everyone at the table.

"Merry Christmas," she finally said. "Merry Christmas!"

"Merry Christmas," they shouted back.

"Now can we cut the cake?" Frankie asked.

Maggie laughed again. "Yes! Yes, let's do. Let's cut the Dundee cake."

Miss Amelia's Dundee Cake Recipe

I read several Dundee cake recipes and made up a version for this book. We actually have made the cake and it is delicious! However, please feel free to adapt the recipe as you feel necessary. – J.R. Stafford

2 cups flour
1 1/3 cups granulated sugar
4 eggs
¾ cup blanched almonds
1 cup butter
1 tsp baking powder
1 cup raisins
1 cup currants
1 cup white raisins
1 tbsp grated orange rind
1 tbsp grated lemon rind
½ cup Scotch whiskey
2 tbsp orange marmalade or apricot jam
Piece of cheesecloth

Instructions

Mix together butter and orange and lemon rinds
Add marmalade or apricot jam
Add sugar and beat until light and creamy
Add eggs one at a time with 1 tbsp of flour per egg and beat each egg thoroughly before adding the next
Add raisins and currants
Sift remaining flour and baking powder together and fold into wet mixture
Spoon mixture into a lightly greased cake pan lined with parchment paper
Use the back of a spoon to spread mixture evenly

Janet R. Stafford

Arrange the almonds in concentric circles so that their points face the center of the pan, but put them on lightly (don't press them down or else they'll disappear into the cake!)

Bake at 325 F for 1½ hours or until a cake tester comes out clean. You may check the cake's progress after about an hour. If it is getting too brown, put a piece of foil on top so it will cook thoroughly without burning

Remove from oven and let cool in cake pan

Once cake is cool, remove from pan

Dampen cheesecloth with water and then pour whiskey over it

Wrap cake in the cheesecloth and place in a cake tin. (The whiskey soaked cheesecloth will keep the cake from drying out.)

About the Author

Janet Stafford is a Jersey girl, book lover and lifelong scribbler. She readily confesses to being overly-educated, having received a B.A. in Asian Studies from Seton Hall University, as well as a Master of Divinity degree and a Ph.D. in North American Religion and Culture from Drew University. Having answered a call to vocational, but non-ordained ministry, Janet has served six United Methodist Churches, working in spiritual formation, communications, and ministries with children, youth, and families. She also was an adjunct professor for six years, teaching college classes in interdisciplinary studies and world history.

Writing, history, and religion came together for Janet when she authored *Saint Maggie*, an historical novel set in 1860-61 and based on a research paper written during her Ph.D. studies. She thought the book would be a single novel, but kept hearing readers ask, "What happens next?" In response, Janet created a series that follows the unconventional family from the first book through three other novels and three short stories, all set in the traumatic years of the American Civil War.

Janet also ventured into the contemporary romance genre, going closer to home (the church) for her source material. *Heart Soul & Rock 'n' Roll* tells the story of 40-year-old Lindsay Mitchell, who led a rock band in college but for the past fifteen years has worked as an assistant minister. Besieged by mid-life crisis, Lins wonders if perhaps she isn't called to something new. But could that "something new" be a relationship with Neil, a man with a messy life and a bar band called the Jersey Reapers?

www.ingramcontent.com/pod-product-compliance
Lightning Source LLC
Chambersburg PA
CBHW050917120626
46552CB00004B/1613